Rose & Alva

THE ROSE
CHAPTER BOOK COLLECTION

Adapted from the Rose Years books
by Roger Lea MacBride
Illustrated by Doris Ettlinger

LITTLE HOUSE

Rose #3

Rose & Alva

ADAPTED FROM THE ROSE YEARS BOOKS BY

Roger Lea MacBride

ILLUSTRATED BY

Doris Ettlinger

HarperTrophy®
A Division of HarperCollinsPublishers

Adaptation by Heather Henson.

HarperCollins®, ▰®, Little House®, Harper Trophy®, and The Rose Years™
are trademarks of HarperCollins Publishers Inc.

Rose & Alva
Text adapted from *Little House on Rocky Ridge*,
text copyright 1993 by Roger Lea MacBride; *Little Farm in the Ozarks*,
text copyright 1994 by Roger Lea MacBride; *In the Land of the Big Red Apple*,
text copyright 1995 by Roger Lea MacBride; *On the Other Side of the Hill*,
text copyright 1995 by Roger Lea MacBride.
Illustrations by Doris Ettlinger
Illustrations copyright © 2000 by Renée Graef
Copyright © 2000 by HarperCollins Publishers

Library of Congress Cataloging-in-Publication Data
MacBride, Roger Lea.
   Rose & Alva : adapted from the Rose years books / by Roger Lea
MacBride ; illustrated by Doris Ettlinger.
     p.   cm. — (A Little house chapter book)
   Summary: Rose meets a girl named Alva, a neighbor at her Missouri farm,
and together they explore the hills, pick pokeweed, explore a cave, and have
other adventures in the Ozark Mountains.
   ISBN 0-06-442095-7 (pbk.) — ISBN 0-06-028158-8 (lib. bdg.)
   1. Lane, Rose Wilder, 1886–1968—Juvenile fiction. [1. Lane, Rose Wilder,
1886–1968—Fiction. 2. Wilder, Laura Ingalls, 1867–1957—Family—Fiction.
3. Farm life—Missouri—Fiction. 4. Missouri—Fiction.] I. Title: Rose and
Alva. II. Ettlinger, Doris, ill. III. Title. III. Series.
PZ7.M478275Ro 2000   99-39845
[Fic]—dc21   CIP
                                                                    AC

❖

First Harper Trophy edition, 2000

Contents

CHAPTER 1

A New Friend

Rose Wilder lived in a little log cabin in the Ozark Mountains of Missouri. Rose and her mama and papa had moved to their new farm in Missouri from South Dakota.

Mama named the new farm Rocky Ridge because the land was very rocky. They were going to grow apple trees on the farm, but the trees were all very small. It would be many years before they had an apple crop to sell. So, for now, Mama and Papa were making do with what they had.

Rose was always busy helping Mama and Papa around the farm. But on Sundays, she was allowed to play. She loved to explore in the woods around the farm with her little dog, Fido.

One Sunday after dinner, Rose decided to follow the little stream that ran near their log cabin to see where it went. She walked down a hill and through a thick patch of trees. Fido stayed close at her heels, until he heard a rustling sound. Then he disappeared into the bushes.

At the bottom of the hill, the little stream turned into a bigger creek. Rose walked along the banks until she came to a tree she had never seen before. The tree had yellow and white fruits the size of plums hanging from its branches. A few of the fruits had fallen and smashed on the ground. The air around the tree smelled sweet. Honeybees buzzed everywhere.

Rose knew she shouldn't eat the fruit without asking Mama first. But she thought that if the bees liked it, she would like it, too.

She bent down and touched her finger to one of the fallen fruits. The juice tasted sweet, almost as sweet as a plum. So she stood up and picked a beautiful yellow-orange fruit from the tree. Slowly she took a small bite.

At first, the taste was nothing—not sweet, but not tart, either. It was just a bit crunchy. Then she felt a strange roughness in her mouth. Her tongue began to shrivel. Her whole mouth turned dry as dust.

It was the worst thing Rose had ever tasted! She began to cough. Tears welled up in her eyes. She thought she was being poisoned.

Then she heard laughter. She whirled around and saw a freckle-faced girl standing nearby. The girl was about her size, and she was wearing a bright-yellow calico dress. Her fiery red hair was pulled into pigtails. Her eyes were very blue. She was staring hard at Rose.

"Your face looks like my pa's tobacco pouch," the girl said in a mocking voice.

"Serves you right, I guess. Those are my pa's persimmons."

Rose wanted to spit out the horrible-tasting fruit. But her mouth was too dry to spit. So she pulled it out with her finger. After a few moments her mouth began to feel right again.

Now Rose's face blazed hot. She was embarrassed and angry. But she tried to remember her manners.

"I'm sorry," she stammered. "I didn't know it was your tree."

"Where're you from?" the girl asked, but she didn't wait for Rose to answer. "You ain't from around here, or you'd of knowed better than to eat a green persimmon. Are you from that wagon in the hollow over yonder? My pa don't like drifters. He won't like it one bit if I tell him covered-wagon folks was

5

stealing his persimmons."

Rose was shocked. She didn't like what the girl was saying. But she knew she shouldn't have been taking what belonged to someone else.

"We aren't drifters," Rose said finally. "We live here. That's our farm. Right back there."

"Well, then," the girl said, giving Rose a friendly smile. "That's a different story. Why didn't you say so? We're neighbors. My pa says you got to be neighborly to neighbors. Where'd you say your farm's at?"

"Up there," Rose said, pointing up the hill. "We just moved into our house."

"Well, this is my pa's place, on this side of Fry Creek." The girl swung her arms out proudly. "I've lived here my whole life, eight years. I'm the baby. How old are you?"

6

"I'll be eight in December," Rose answered. "But I'm the only one."

"I got six brothers and sisters," the girl continued. "My two big sisters don't like farm work much. They help my ma with the cookin' and house chores. But I like helpin' my pa in the barn and out in the fields. My pa says I'm the best son a man could ever hope for." The girl stopped talking and grinned. Then she asked, "What's your name?"

"Rose. Rose Wilder. I came with my mama and papa from South Dakota."

"South Dakota? What's it like there?" the girl asked.

"It's prairie," Rose explained. "It's all grass. And windy. And there aren't any trees."

"No trees!" the girl shouted. "Where do the birds put their nests? What about squirrels? You mean you got no squirrels there?"

"No," Rose replied.

"How 'bout coons and possums?"

"No," Rose said again. "But there are jackrabbits and gophers."

The girl shook her head and laughed. Then she told Rose about persimmons.

"These ain't ripe yet," she explained, showing Rose a persimmon like the one she had bitten into. It was firm, and the color was lighter than the others. "You cain't eat 'em till they get soft."

The girl reached into the tree and picked another persimmon.

"Here's a real good ripe one. See?" She held it out for Rose. "It's dark and kind of mushy. My ma cooks them in pudding. Smack down on it."

Rose took a small bite. This time her

8

mouth filled with sweet juice. Rose had never tasted anything like it before. She ate all of the delicious fruit, spitting out the slimy brown seeds.

After a little while, the girl squinted up at the sky.

"Well, I got to go," she said. "Looks like rain, and I got to help Pa with the milking. I'll see you around."

"Good-bye," Rose said, waving. Then she remembered something. "Wait!" she called. "What's your name?"

"Alva. Alva Stubbins." The girl grinned and waved. "See you, Rose."

Rose gathered a few ripe persimmons in her skirt. Then she raced to get home before the rain started. She couldn't wait to show Mama the new fruit and tell her about her new friend.

CHAPTER 2

The Deer Rub

For the rest of the week, Rose thought about Alva Stubbins as she went about her chores. She hoped she would see her again soon.

Finally on Sunday, Rose had just finished her morning chores when she saw someone coming through the woods. The person was wearing overalls and a boy's straw hat. Rose didn't know who it was at first. But then she saw one fiery red pigtail peeking out from under the hat brim.

"Alva!" Rose shouted happily.

"Say, Rose!" Alva called out. "I'm going to see a deer rub. Come on, I'll show you."

"What's a deer rub?" Rose asked.

"You never seen a deer rub?" Alva cried. "Well, come on then."

Rose ran to ask Mama if she could go, and then she followed Alva into the woods. Fido scampered beside them as they walked along streams and climbed hills. When they reached a stream that ran between two hills, Alva stopped and pointed at the water.

"Look!" she said. "A crawdad!"

Alva knelt down beside the stream and stared at something. She reached out her hand very slowly. Fido stood beside Alva. He watched the water, his head cocked to one side.

Suddenly, Alva's hand darted into the water. Fido barked. In a second Alva was holding something right in front of Rose's face.

It was an ugly brown creature about two inches long, dripping wet. Its bulgy eyes came out of its head on stalks. Its two rows of little legs crawled in the air. Its scaly tail curled.

"It's trying to bite!" Rose squealed.

The creature's two front legs were claws, snapping at the air.

12

"It's a crawdad," said Alva. "Watch this." With her other hand she picked up a little twig. The creature reached out a claw and cut the little twig in two!

Alva laughed and put the crawdad back into the stream.

"They're good to eat," Alva explained. "We ought to catch ourselves a mess and cook 'em up sometime."

Rose didn't say so, but she didn't think she would want to eat such an ugly-looking thing.

Soon they came to a grove of small trees. On some of the trees, the bark had been rubbed off in streaks. Alva said that this was the deer rub.

"The deer comes and rubs his baby horns, to make them strong," Alva explained.

They waited quietly behind some

13

bushes, but they didn't see any deer.

So Alva showed Rose raccoon tracks, which looked like a child's handprints. And she showed her holes in the ground where foxes slept.

As they walked, Fido ran all through the woods. He stuck his nose into rotting logs and fox dens and raccoon tracks.

Alva showed Rose tracks where civet cats had walked in the mud.

"A civet cat is like a skunk," Alva explained. "Only they ain't so waddly. And you don't get much for the fur."

Alva seemed to know about all the animals in the forest. She knew about hunting, and she knew about trapping. She even had her own money that she earned from trapping and selling furs.

"I got seventy cents all saved up," Alva said proudly. "You can come to my

 14

house and look at it."

Rose hoped she would be able to go to Alva's house sometime soon. She liked Alva. And she was having so much fun, she wished the morning would never end. But she knew it must be close to dinnertime, and Mama expected her back.

"I think I should go home now," Rose said, looking around the forest. "We aren't lost, are we?"

"You won't never get lost, long as you're around me." Alva laughed. "I know my way in these hill better'n anybody."

As they neared Rocky Ridge Farm, Rose heard the faraway sound of a bell.

"There's my ma, calling dinner!" Alva yelled. "I got to go."

"Good-bye, Alva!" Rose shouted. She watched as Alva raced off down the hill, her red braids flying behind her. Alva was different from any girl Rose had ever met. She was much more fun than the polite girls Rose had played with back home in South Dakota.

CHAPTER 3

The Cave

After that Alva stopped by almost every Sunday to see if Rose could play. They played in the woods or by the creek. Sometimes they made little houses out of rocks. Other times they made a little pond in the creek so they could watch the fish and crawdads swim around.

One Sunday Alva showed Rose a cave. It was an enormous hole deep in the side of a hill near the farm. A little stream trickled out of its dark mouth. From inside, Rose could hear the hollow sound

17

of dripping water.

"What's in there?" Rose asked in a whisper.

"Things you ain't never seen," Alva answered. "Crickets that look like bumblebees. Bats. And sometimes even wild hogs."

"Hogs?" Rose cried. She had seen wild

hogs in the orchard. They were mean, and Papa had told her to stay away from them.

"Yep," Alva replied. "They live in caves sometimes."

"Are there hogs in there now?" Rose gulped.

"Probably not," said Alva. "If any hogs live here, they're out eating acorns."

Alva pulled on Rose's arm.

"Come on," she said, walking into the cave. "Do you want to see or not? It's nothing to be afraid of. I come here plenty."

Rose followed Alva into a dark, empty room with a high ceiling. The air was cooler inside.

"It makes your voice echo," said Rose. She shouted out, "Hello!" From somewhere deep inside the cave Rose heard a tiny voice answer, "Hello!"

"Listen to this," said Alva, and she screamed at the top of her lungs. The cave made her voice sound so big and scary that Rose started screaming, too. Then they both laughed until they couldn't breathe.

Slowly, they started to walk farther into the cave. The sound of falling water grew louder. The floor was covered with rocks and stones.

Rose was a little scared, but Alva pulled her on.

"Come on," Alva said. "If them hogs was here, they'd of showed theirselves. Or you'd of smelled them. There ain't no hog tracks, anyway."

The cave became smaller. Soon it was like a long narrow tunnel, just tall enough for them to stand up. The light from outside grew dimmer.

A little stream ran down the middle of

 20

the tunnel. The water was icy on Rose's bare feet, so she walked on a muddy ledge beside the stream. Her feet made sucking sounds when she picked them up. The rough stone wall was cool and damp. The air felt clammy.

Rose and Alva kept going farther into the cave until the darkness seemed to swallow them up.

"I can't see anything," Rose said. Her voice sounded small and muffled, as if the walls were soaking it up. "I think we should go back."

Rose turned around to find the opening of the cave. She let out a little gasp. The light from the cave's mouth was just a pale smudge in the distance.

Just then the deep silence was broken by a loud SPLASH!

"What was that?" Rose whispered.

"Did you do that?"

"Not me," Alva said in a shaky voice.

Rose's legs prickled with fear. She stood still, staring into the blackness. She listened.

There was another SPLASH, followed by a *splash-splash-splash-splish*. Then they heard a loud grunt.

"Uh-oh," Alva said.

Without another thought, Rose began to run. She didn't care about the cold water now. She ran wherever her feet landed. She heard Alva running behind her. But then she tripped and fell, scraping her hands on the rocks. She felt Alva flying past her.

In a flash, Rose was up and running again. Finally she burst out through the opening. She had to squint against the bright sunlight. But she didn't stop until she caught up with Alva in the woods.

Alva was doubled over, trying to catch her breath. Rose fell on the ground beside her. She gulped in the fresh, dry air. It smelled sweet and clean after the dampness of the cave. The woods were peaceful and safe.

Rose's legs trembled and her lungs burned. Her palms were raw from the fall. But she started giggling, and Alva began to giggle, too.

"What was that sound?" Rose asked finally, looking back toward the cave. "Was it a hog?"

"Naw," Alva said. "Maybe a bobcat or a raccoon. Raccoons like to splash in the water."

Rose and Alva went to the creek. They washed the mud off their hands and dresses. Then they walked slowly back to the farm. Rose thought about the cave as they went. It had been scary, but it had also been exciting. She knew there would always be fun things to do as long as Alva was around.

CHAPTER 4

Sassafras and Pokeweed

Soon the leaves began to fade in the woods around Rocky Ridge Farm. The weather turned chilly. Rose shivered as she went about her chores in the morning.

Rose knew that one of the reasons Mama and Papa had come to Missouri was because the planting season was long and the winters were short. Back in South Dakota, the winters had been very hard. Cold winds howled across the prairie night

25

and day. The snow came in great blizzards. Here in Missouri, there was cold and snow, but it didn't last as long.

Still, once winter settled in, Rose saw Alva only now and then. Rose was too busy helping Mama around the house and learning her lessons.

Rose missed Alva, but she also had a new friend. Swiney Baird was about the same age as Rose. Papa had found him stealing eggs from their henhouse one night. Swiney didn't have a mother or father. They had died years before. He lived with his older brother, Abe, who was often too busy trying to make a living to look after Swiney. Now Abe worked for Papa, helping him around the farm. Swiney helped, too.

When March came, the snow melted and the ground thawed. Papa began to plow up the garden and the fields.

The ground was full of roots and rocks. Mama, Rose, and Swiney picked up all the rocks and stones and carried them out of the way of Papa's plow.

Picking up rocks was hard work. Mud got on Rose's clothes and under her nails. Her back ached from stooping over, and her hands became chapped.

One day while Rose was resting, she caught sight of Alva coming through the woods.

"Alva!" Rose shouted happily.

"Hello, Rose!" Alva shouted back. Then she said politely, "Hello, Mrs. Wilder."

"What a pleasant surprise." Mama smiled. "What brings you visiting?"

"My ma sent me over with some sassafras," Alva said. She handed Mama a bundle of small tree roots tied up with a string. Rose could smell a strong odor coming from the bundle.

"That's very nice," Mama said, turning the bundle over in her hand. "But I don't know what to do with it."

"It makes tea," Swiney piped up. "To thin your blood. Everybody takes sassafras tea in the spring."

Alva frowned at Swiney. "Yes," she said. "It perks your blood up when it gets too thick in the winter."

"This is Swiney Baird," Rose said. "His big brother Abe is my papa's new hired man."

Alva looked at Swiney, but she did not say anything. Then she turned back toward Mama. "Can Rose come and play a spell?" she asked. "I found some poke-weed down by Wolf Creek. We could pick you a mess for salad."

"Pokeweed?" said Mama.

"It's greens," Swiney piped up again. "We always eat greens in the spring."

"I don't see why not." Mama nodded. "Are you sure you know what's good to eat, and what isn't?"

"Yes, ma'am," Alva said. "I help my ma with the picking every year. We ain't never got sick yet."

Rose took a pail from the house and walked to Wolf Creek with Alva. Mama said Swiney could go, too, so he trailed behind them.

At Wolf Creek, Alva showed Rose a clump of pokeweed. Rose had seen green leaves pushing up here and there in the forest, but she hadn't known which ones she could eat.

"You take the little soft leaves," Alva

explained. "But not the root. That's the bad part."

"I got a knife, so I'll be the cutter," Swiney said loudly. He took out his knife and started to sharpen it.

"Who says?" Alva cried. "We don't need no cutter anyway. We can just tear them off."

"Can not!" Swiney shouted.

"Can too!" Alva shouted back. "You can just go find your own poke and cut it if you like. We don't care."

"Humph!" Swiney grumbled. He walked off and began carving his name in the trunk of a tree.

Rose and Alva talked and laughed as they picked greens. It felt so good to be together again in the warm sunshine.

Alva showed Rose other greens that were good to eat, too. There was lamb'squarter and cow parsley. On the edge of the creek, they found watercress.

"Try it," said Alva. "It's real good."

Rose pulled up some of the tiny leaves and put them in her mouth. It tasted fresh and tangy, like radishes.

Just then Swiney called out to them.

"Watch me! Look! Bet you can't do this!" he shouted.

Rose turned to see Swiney standing on top of a fence. As soon as he knew they were watching, he began to walk shakily along the top rail.

"That's nothing. We don't care, anyway," Alva sniffed.

Just as Swiney got to the end of the fence, he tried to turn around. But he lost his balance and fell, headfirst.

Rose gasped, but just before Swiney's head hit the ground, one of his pant legs got tangled in the fence. He stopped short, hanging upside down above the ground.

"Ow!" he screamed. "I'm stuck!" He wriggled and tried to lift himself back up with his arms. He twisted and turned and huffed and kicked. But no matter how hard he tried, he couldn't unstick himself. His face turned bright red.

"Ha, ha, ha," Alva laughed, pointing at him while he struggled upside down. "I guess I know why they call you Swiney. You got your snout into everything."

Rose giggled. She hadn't thought of it before, but Swiney really did get into trouble like an old hog.

"Get me down," Swiney cried. His face puckered up. "Help me!"

"Maybe we ought to just leave him there," Alva said, putting her hands on her

hips. "It would serve him right, sticking his swiney snout into everything. Whiney Swiney!" she taunted.

"No," Rose said. She didn't like Swiney as well as she liked Alva, and she couldn't help but laugh at how foolish he looked. But Rose could never be truly mean. Especially not to poor Swiney, who had no mother and father.

"Come and help," she said to Alva.

Together they lifted Swiney up until his pant leg came loose. Then he fell to the ground in a heap, like a pile of old clothes.

Swiney got up and brushed himself off. His face was red and angry.

"Are you all right?" Rose asked.

"Awww, never mind!" Swiney yelled. He stomped off toward the house.

Rose watched after him, and then

went back to picking greens with Alva. When the bucket was full, Alva said she had to go. But she promised to come more often now that spring was here.

That evening, Mama cut the sassafras roots into short pieces. Then she put them in a big kettle of water to simmer. The house quickly filled with a strong, spicy smell.

They sat down to a dinner of greens and corn bread. The greens tasted so good. Rose was tired of the beans and salt pork they had eaten all winter long.

When the dishes were washed and put away, Mama served the sassafras tea. Rose liked it better than grown-up tea.

Sassafras tea was another amazing thing Rose learned from Alva. She couldn't imagine what Alva would teach her next!

CHAPTER 5

Alva's House

When summer came, the woods around the little log cabin bloomed with beautiful wildflowers. The birds darted through the trees, chirping happily. And the squirrels scurried about, nesting and feeding their young.

Abe and Swiney did not come to help very often now. They were busy helping another neighbor plant and hoe his crops.

One morning Rose was helping Mama scrub the wash in the warm sunshine when she saw Alva tramping up the hill.

She said she had come to invite Rose to her house for dinner. Rose had not been to Alva's house yet. She begged Mama to let her go.

"Very well," said Mama with a smile. "Remember your manners, and thank Mrs. Stubbins. I will expect you home in time for evening chores."

Rose and Alva ran all the way through the woods. When they reached the Stubbinses' farm, Rose saw that Alva's house was made of logs, just like hers. But Alva's house was very big, with two whole floors of rooms. And there was a summer kitchen nearby, and a little smokehouse.

In the barnyard there were dozens of hens scratching in the dirt. Geese walked on the banks of a small creek. Ducks swam in a little pond near the milkhouse. Pigs were in the woods nearby. And there was a pasture with a herd of cows, and horses and mules, too.

Rose looked all around, wide-eyed. She had not known that Alva's family was so rich.

"Howdy, Rose," Mrs. Stubbins called when Alva led Rose into the kitchen. "We're right proud to welcome you. It's about time you was a-visiting. Alva's all the time bragging about you."

Dinner was a merry feast. Rose sat next to Alva at a long table, with Alva's six brothers and sisters, Mr. and Mrs. Stubbins, and a hired hand. Everyone talked and laughed as they ate.

Mrs. Stubbins brought in a big plate of fried chicken and another plate of ham. There were boiled potatoes and biscuits with fresh butter. And there was fresh milk to drink. Rose couldn't remember when she had eaten so well.

"How do you find it here in the Ozarks?" asked Effie, who was Alva's oldest sister.

"I like it very much, thank you," Rose said politely. "Except for snakes and wild hogs."

Everyone laughed.

"Yep, we got ourselves a mess of snakes and other pests in these hills," said Mr. Stubbins. "You young 'uns got to watch out, running around barefoot all summer. Most snakes are harmless. But we got some that are right poisonous."

"Yes, sir," Rose gulped.

When everyone had eaten their fill, Mrs. Stubbins began to clear the dishes. It was time for the grown-ups to go back to work.

"Thank you, Mrs. Stubbins," Rose

said. "It was a very good dinner."

"Don't even mention it," Mrs. Stubbins replied. "You come any old time you please. And tell your ma and pa to come a-visiting, too. There's always room at our table for good neighbors."

Rose began to help with the dishes.

"You ain't got to do that," said Alva. "My sisters do the washing up. Come on. I'll show you around our farm."

Rose thought Alva was very lucky to have big sisters to help with the chores. At home Rose helped with everything. She was almost as busy as Mama, all day long.

Alva took Rose into the barn, where a mother cat was nursing her kittens. The kittens were as tiny as mice. They paddled her with their little paws.

Rose picked one up and cuddled it in

 40

the palm of her hand. The kitten nosed between her fingers. It mewed softly.

"When they get older you can have one, Rose," Alva said.

"Could I?" Rose asked, her voice barely a whisper.

"Pa said we got too many cats," Alva said. "Which one do you want?"

Rose looked down at the tiny kittens. They all looked the same, with striped orange fur on their backs and white fur on their bellies. Their tiny eyes were shut tight, and their small, baby ears lay close to their heads. Their short, pointy tails stood straight up. Only one had a black foot, and it was a little smaller than the rest.

"That one," said Rose. "I like that one because I can tell it from the others."

"I'll tell Pa. When he says it's old enough, you can come and take it," Alva said.

Rose clapped her hands with joy. "Thank you, Alva! Thank you so much."

Together Rose and Alva played away the rest of the afternoon. They made mud pies and left them to bake in the warm sun. Then they tried to follow some bees so they could find their nest. But they lost track of the bees in the woods.

At last it was time for Rose to go home. She went back to the barn to peek at her kitten one last time. She decided to name it Blackfoot.

Rose thanked Alva for everything. Then she ran through the woods, full of excitement. When she reached home, she told Mama all about the Stubbinses' farm. Then she told her about the kitten.

Mama smiled up from her ironing. "We certainly could use a good mouser," she said. "When the crops come in this fall, we will need a cat to keep the rats and mice out of them."

Rose clapped her hands together. She felt so happy. It had been such a wonderful day. She wished she could visit Alva's house more often.

But any more visits would have to wait. Rose was starting school the very next week. She had forgotten all about it until Mama reminded her.

Rose had loved her school in South Dakota. But she didn't know if she would like it in Missouri. She knew Alva wouldn't be there. Alva's folks didn't think she needed to go to school. They let her work around the farm instead.

As Rose got ready for bed that night, she thought about being the new girl in a classroom full of strangers, and her stomach felt all fluttery inside. Suddenly she wished with all her heart she could stay home from school, just like Alva.

CHAPTER 6

Sneaking Off

On the first day of school, Rose got up extra early. She did all her chores and ate her breakfast. Then she put on the new dress Mama made for her. It was blue and lavender gingham with a little lace collar.

Usually a new dress made Rose feel good. But today she felt terrible. She thought of Alva and Blackfoot, and her heart ached.

At school the terrible feeling did not go away. Professor Kay was nice, but his

45

lessons were dull. Rose did not make any friends. The town girls were rude. And the country girls did not seem very friendly, either.

On the second morning of school, Rose woke with that same terrible feeling. She wanted to beg Mama to stay home, but she knew it would do no good. Mama had been a schoolteacher before she married Papa. Rose knew how important school was to Mama.

All morning long, Rose sat at her desk and stared out the window while the other students recited their lessons. She wondered what Alva was doing that very minute. She wondered if the little kittens had opened their eyes yet.

When noon finally came, Rose ate her dinner quickly. She put her dinner pail back on the shelf in the classroom.

Then she left school.

Rose ran all the way to Alva's house. She knew she must hurry if she was going to be back in time for afternoon lessons.

When she reached the Stubbinses' yard, Alva was standing on the porch.

"How come you ain't in school?" Alva asked in surprise.

"I am," said Rose. "I just wanted to see Blackfoot."

"Come on, then." Alva laughed. "Their little eyes are open now."

Sure enough, all the kittens' eyes were wide open. They had grown so much in just a week. Now they played with one another, pouncing and kicking their tiny feet.

Rose picked up Blackfoot. He climbed up onto her shoulder and batted at her hair. Then he mewed softly to get down.

"Oh, Alva." Rose sighed. "I hate school so."

"I'm glad my ma and pa don't make me go to no school," said Alva. "My pa says you don't need no schooling to know how to milk cows and hoe corn. I just know I couldn't sit in those old seats for a minute."

Rose took one more look at the kittens. Then she followed Alva outside to get a drink at the spring.

"Look, Rose!" Alva shouted. "There are the bees again! Let's follow them and see if we can find the nest."

"I don't think I should," said Rose uncertainly. "I might be late for school."

"We won't go far," Alva said. "Come on, there goes one now."

Alva took off across the field after the bee, and Rose followed.

"I can still see it!" Alva shouted. But when they were deep in the woods, Alva lost sight of it.

On the way back to the house, they stopped to watch two colts racing across the pasture. Then they found a blackberry patch. They plucked and ate all the berries they could find.

Rose remembered school, but she was sure she still had time to get back. She had not heard the bell, and it wasn't far if she ran.

Along the creek they stopped to watch the crawdads. Blue dragonflies hovered over the water, darting to catch bugs.

Finally, Rose knew she had better go. She said good-bye to Alva and ran all the way back to school.

When she got to the top of the hill overlooking the schoolhouse, she stopped and stared. The schoolyard was empty! None of the children's horses were in the shed.

But then she saw one wagon near the front door. Her stomach flip-flopped. She knew it was Mama and Papa's wagon.

Rose walked slowly down the hill. She trembled as she climbed the steps one at a time. Her feet were as heavy as stones.

When she opened the classroom door, Mama, Papa, and Professor Kay all turned to look at her. Mama's face was very stern.

"Where have you been?" Mama asked, and her voice had never sounded so angry.

Rose could think of nothing to say. She stared at the floor.

"Professor Kay dismissed the class an hour ago," Mama continued. "Papa and I have been worried sick."

"I went to Alva's," Rose said meekly. "I'm sorry, Mama. I only wanted to see the kitten. I didn't know I would be so long."

Mama shook her head. "To think, you could have been lying hurt somewhere!"

Papa cleared his throat. "Now, Bess," he said gently. "She's here now, safe and sound. Just some foolishness. But you mustn't ever do anything like that again, Rose."

"Yes, Papa," Rose said softly, and she meant it with all her heart. She felt like crying. She hated making Mama and Papa worry.

For the rest of the week, Rose had to stay inside the classroom during recess and dinner. She still missed Alva, but slowly she began to make some new friends. And Professor Kay allowed her to read the storybooks he kept on a special shelf.

On Sunday Alva came to visit. She was carrying a sack that meowed loudly. When she opened it, Blackfoot jumped out.

The kitten shook himself, blinking in the bright light. Then he rubbed against Rose's leg and meowed happily.

"He remembers me!" Rose cried.

For the rest of the morning, Rose and Alva played with Blackfoot. Rose told Alva about school, and Alva told Rose about the things she had been doing on the farm.

Rose didn't mind school so much anymore. But she was glad it was Sunday, and she was glad to be with Alva.

CHAPTER 7

Pressing Cider

All during the next year, when Rose wasn't in school, she helped Mama and Papa on Rocky Ridge. Soon the little farm began to grow.

Papa cleared more land for more apple trees and corn and oats. He cleared a grazing pasture for the two horses, the two mules, and the new cow and calf. He even built a new, bigger house for Mama and Rose.

Farming was hard work, and it seemed to Rose like she was always tired. But the days went quickly, and soon it was harvest time again.

One crisp fall day, Papa came home with a wagonload of apples from an orchard nearby. Rose knew that they would have to buy apples from other farmers for several years, until their own trees were big enough. But she didn't know what Papa was going to do with all the apples in his wagon.

"These aren't eating apples," Papa explained. "We're taking them to the Stubbinses' for a cider pressing."

Rose squealed with delight. She was always happy to go to Alva's.

Papa helped Mama and Rose into the wagon, and they took off down the road. As soon as they reached the Stubbinses' farm, Rose could smell the sweet scent of apples.

The minute the wagon stopped, Rose jumped down and ran into the barn. There were baskets of apples everywhere. A group of people were standing around a tall machine with a big iron wheel on top. Papa had told Rose that several families were coming to use Mr. Stubbins's press that day. In return, they would give Mr. Stubbins some of their cider.

Rose took a deep breath. The air was thick and tangy. Finally, she saw Alva sitting in the corner of the barn, surrounded by baskets of apples.

"What are you doing?" Rose asked, running up to her.

Alva told her that she was cutting off the bruised parts of the apples before they went into the machine.

Rose watched Alva for a while. "I never saw a cider pressing before," she said.

 56

Alva put down her paring knife. She grabbed Rose's hand and took her over to the press.

The press was a wooden machine that stood on legs. Mr. Stubbins was dumping apples into a box on the top. Alva said that was called the hopper.

Another man cranked a handle that turned a spiky metal wheel under the hopper. The wheel smashed up the apples and then spat them into a wooden barrel with slats in the bottom.

When the barrel was full, the men slid it under the press. They turned another big metal wheel on top. The press came slowly down, squashing the apples even more. Juice began to pour between the slats as the press smashed the apples flatter and flatter. The juice ran into a chute and out a small hole into a bucket.

All the grown-ups standing around the machine had brought their own tin cups to taste the cider. Rose didn't have a cup, but Alva had one in the pocket of her apron. She quickly stuck it in the foamy brown stream of cider and caught a cupful.

"Here," Alva said, holding it out to Rose. "Have a drink."

Rose took a big, long gulp. The cider was smooth and sweet. It was the best she had ever tasted.

"C'mon," Alva said. "I got to finish the apples. We can talk while I'm a-cutting."

Rose sat down on the barn floor. She watched Alva's quick hands carve out the brown places on the apples. As she worked, Alva told Rose how she had been chased by a wolf the other night.

"After supper," Alva began, "Mama sent me over to the Deavers' with a pail of milk because their cow had died. I was a-walking through the woods over past the railroad tracks, and I heared a dog a-barking. But it weren't like no dog I ever heared afore. Then I heared it a-howling, and I knowed it weren't no dog at all. It was a wolf!"

Rose could feel the hair rise on the

back of her neck. She stared at Alva with eyes wide open.

"So I started a-walking fast as I could, a-being careful for the milk not to spill," Alva continued. "But that old wolf was a-coming, Rose. I heared him bark real close. I stopped and listened. At first, all I could hear was my own heart a-drumming fast as a rabbit's. But then, plain as anything, I heared its feet a-running in the leaves."

"What did you do?" Rose squealed. She could feel her own heart pounding, too.

"I ran!" Alva shouted. "I ran with all my might, a-spilling milk all over. Finally I seen a bit of yellow light from the Deavers' windows. But when I got near the house, I stubbed my foot and fell. A big gulp of milk spilled out. Lickity split

60

I got up and ran to the door and banged on it."

Alva paused to catch her breath, and Rose waited to hear what happened next.

"Afore Missus Deavers could come and open the door," Alva went on, "I looked back. There was that old wolf a-lapping up the milk, his bushy tail a-wagging like an old dog. Then Mr. Deavers's hunting dogs took up a-yapping and the wolf ran off."

"How did you get home?" Rose asked.

Alva grabbed the last apple from the bottom of the basket. She began hacking away at it.

"Mr. Deavers let his dogs loose on the wolf, and he rode me home on his horse. My papa and him went out three nights a-tracking it, but they never did see it. Papa said it was probably a lone wolf, a-looking for its pack, and got hungry when it smelled the milk."

Rose tingled all over. She couldn't imagine anything as scary as being chased by a wolf. She thought Alva had been very brave.

For the rest of the day, Rose and Alva played together in the barn. When all the apples had been pressed, everyone stood around. They talked and laughed and took turns tasting one another's cider.

Rose was surprised to find that each kind of apple had a different flavor. Some were smooth and sweet. Others were so strong and sour they made her mouth pucker.

When everyone was getting ready to leave, Alva asked if Rose could come play on Sunday. Mama said she could, as long as Rose was back in time for her evening chores.

On the way home, Rose sat in the wagon-box, leaning her back against the huge barrel of sloshing cider. The cider pressing had been so much fun. And now she had Sunday to look forward to.

CHAPTER 8

Train Tracks

The week seemed to go very slowly. Finally Sunday arrived. After dinner Rose helped Mama with the dishes. Then she dashed out the door and ran through the woods as fast as she could. Alva was waiting for her in the barnyard.

"Take me where you saw the wolf," Rose pleaded.

Alva led the way over a hill and through a little valley to the train tracks at the very edge of the Stubbinses' farm. They climbed up the steep hill to the tracks. Then they stood for a moment to catch their breath. They looked down the silver tracks.

Rose felt a tingle of excitement. Every day she heard the train whistle and the *clickity-clack* of the wheels in the distance. But she had never been this close to the tracks before. She thought about how a big train could come thundering by at any moment.

Alva grabbed Rose's hand and took her to the edge of the woods where she had first heard the wolf. She began to tell the story again. When she got to the part where she tripped and fell, Alva suddenly pointed into the woods. She shouted, "Sakes alive, Rose! It's here!"

Rose screamed and whirled around, but she didn't see a wolf. Then she heard Alva laughing, and she felt her cheeks flush red. Without thinking, Rose turned and shoved Alva to the ground. Alva fell backward with a thud.

Alva looked up in surprise. But then she began to laugh again, rolling in the leaves.

"I'm sorry, Rose," she said between giggles. "I was just a-funning you. You oughta seed your face. I got your goat that time."

Rose didn't like being teased, even by Alva. She turned and walked back toward the train tracks. She could hear Alva following her, but she did not turn around. But as she walked, she stopped feeling so angry.

When she reached the train tracks, she stood still and listened. She heard the faint cry of a whistle in the distance.

"A train's coming!" she yelled.

Alva ran up the slope and stood beside her. Then she knelt down and pressed her ear against the rail.

"You can hear it in the tracks," she said.

Rose knelt down and put her ear against the rail, too. She could hear tiny rumbling noises. She knew those were the sounds of the wheels on the track!

Suddenly the train whistle sounded again—louder this time.

Alva jumped up and began searching for something along the tracks. Then she came running back to Rose.

"Look, I found these." She held out her hand. There were two rusty nails in it. "We can put 'em on the track. When the train comes, it'll mash 'em flat."

Alva laid the nails together on the rail, one across the other, in an X. Then she took Rose's hand. They ran back down the embankment to wait for the train.

Rose heard the tracks give out a pinging noise. In the next instant, the great engine swung into view.

"It's coming awfully fast," Rose cried. She felt her heart begin to race. She squeezed Alva's hand tight.

The engine grew bigger and bigger. It seemed to pick up speed as it got closer. A plume of white steam poured out of the top. Then Rose heard the piercing shriek of the whistle.

In a whirling cloud of dust and leaves, the engine whooshed by. The other cars thundered along behind, rocking from side to side.

It was the loudest noise Rose had ever heard. It was like thunder. Rose opened

her mouth and yelled, but she could barely hear herself above the racket.

The wooden cars rumbled and rattled past in a blur. Rose could just make out people sitting at the windows.

Finally, the last car whizzed by. Rose saw two little girls in white dresses standing in the rear door, waving at them.

Then the train was gone, disappearing around the hill.

"Ow!" Alva laughed. "Let go of my hand, Rose. You're a-hurting it."

Rose giggled and rushed up the hill after Alva. She saw that the nails had been smashed flat against the track. They were now one piece of metal, forming an X.

Alva waited for the metal to cool, and then she gave the X to Rose. She said she was sorry for scaring Rose before. And Rose said she was sorry for pushing Alva.

 70

As she walked back home through the woods, Rose thought about all the adventures she had had with Alva. For two years they had tramped every inch of the Ozark hills together, playing in creeks, chasing rabbits, and following bees. At school now Rose had made more friends who were nice and polite. But Rose would never have a friend as exciting as Alva.

Come Home to Little House!

**THE CAROLINE
CHAPTER BOOK COLLECTION**

Adapted from the Caroline Years books
by Maria D. Wilkes
Illustrated by Doris Ettlinger

THE COMPLETE
LAURA CHAPTER BOOK COLLECTION

Adapted from the Little House books
by Laura Ingalls Wilder
Illustrated by Renée Graef and Doris Ettlinger